THE TOURIST BUTCHER

JAMAL OUARIACHI

TRANSLATION BY / *VERTALING DOOR*
SCOTT EMBLEN-JARRETT

The Tourist Butcher
by Jamal Ouariachi

Translated from the Dutch
by Scott Emblen-Jarrett

First published in English
by Strangers Press, Norwich, 2020
(part of UEA Publishing Project)

Printed
by Swallowtail Print, Norwich

All rights reserved
© *2017 Jamal Ouariachi,*
published by Em. Querido's Uitgeverij
Translation
© *Scott Emblen-Jarrett, 2020,*
mentored by David McKay

Editorial team
Nathan Hamilton, David Colmer,
Michele Hutchison, Bas Pauw and Victor Schiferli

Editorial assistance
by Senica Maltese

Cover design and typesetting
by Office of Craig

Main body text is set using Arnhem,
Headings are set in Nord

The rights of Jamal Ouariachi to be identified as the author and Scott Emblen-Jarrett to be identified as the translator of this work have been asserted in accordance with the Copyright, Designs and Patents Act, 1988. This booklet is sold subject to the condition that it shall not, by way of trade or otherwise, be lent, resold, hired out, stored in a retrieval system, or otherwise circulated without the publisher's prior consent in any form of binding or cover other than that in which it is published and without a similar condition including this condition being imposed on the subsequent purchaser.

ISBN-13: 978-1911343301

The Tourist Butcher

CONTENTS

MEMORIES IN TIN FOIL   *5*

THE TOURIST BUTCHER   *17*

strangers press

MEMORIES IN TIN FOIL

A slice of lightly-cooked chestnut mushroom is what it resembled most. It had been stuffed into an inside-out latex glove and wrapped in a piece of kitchen paper.

'What is it exactly?'

Fina burst out laughing at my disgust, clearly taking great pleasure in the face I was pulling. This wasn't the first time this had happened; her sense of humour had a sadistic aspect. A biology student thing.

'Don't you see it?'

All biologists are sadists and take pleasure in the disgust they inspire in others. Their sadism is worn as a badge of honour. Only a biologist could make an incision into a piece of tissue and not wince at the sight of whatever slime or pus or blood oozed out of it. Only a biologist could face the vomit inducing stench emanating from a decomposing whale washed up on a beach. Only a biologist could go rooting around in mammalian faecal matter straight after lunch, and only a biologist would get it into her head to make yoghurt using her own vaginal yeast as an experiment and then serve it to her boyfriend for breakfast. Or maybe only this biologist. No. Sadists all, believe me.

'Brains,' shouted Fina, 'Bra-aaaaa-ains!'

A strange, warm sensation entered my chest, a warmth that reminded me of playing forbidden games as a child; the wavering between good and bad, bad and good; that friction caused this same feeling.

'From a mouse?'

Fina's boyfriend cut the heads off mice and rats for research purposes.

'No, from a human of course. Good luck fitting that in a mouse's head!'

I could now see the cauliflower qualities of a cerebral cortex. But which part? Parietal? Temporal? Just before Fina had come through the door, I had put a frying pan on the hob to start dinner. The idea of frying up a slice of brain just to see what it tasted like drifted into my mind. No. Isn't that how you get hideous diseases like Creutzfeldt-Jakob or something?

'You're joking, right?'

'It's real, no joke. I took it from the lab.'

Fina grabbed a beer from the fridge.

'You said about wanting to see a real-life brain, no? Well, enjoy!'

She picked up a bottle opener from the counter and popped off the bottle top, taking a couple of hearty glugs, before letting out a large belch.

'Oh. That was the last one, by the way. You didn't want one, did you?'

I shook my head, not knowing what to do. My hand was out in front of me, as if I had been begging. The slice of brain sat like an offering. I had indeed said I wanted to see some brains, but only in certain contexts, and after going through the proper channels — like during a biology class practical, and in a lab with a white coat, for example. Such practicals weren't included in my course however; they were for students of medicine and, apparently, biology, but not psychology. Kind of unbelievable, come to think about it, but true.

At that point the closest I had ever come to brains was signing up for an fMRI scan as part of a research study. It was compulsory for first years to participate in faculty research. This was psychology's Achilles' heel: a whole field founded on findings collected from studies involving largely white, largely female, and largely university-educated young people. A fat lot of good these findings would do a retired black man with only a primary-school level of education.

After the fMRI I was given a few photos of my brain in various cross-sections. All these things hidden for so long now visible in an instant. 'You have a beautiful brain', the research assistant told me. Might have just been a line, but I fell for it, blushing with a coy 'Why, thank you'. I was suddenly proud, proud of my beautiful brain. What a moving experience.

I held the piece of brain with such care I began to get cramp in my arm. You'd have thought I was holding a baby.

'You're quite taken with it, aren't you?'

'I think it's magical... beautiful... it's crazy that this was actually in someone's head.'

'Yeah I know, mad, right?'

Fina let out yet another belch and opened the fridge again.

'I'm hungry. You cooking something?'

I spent the rest of the evening in my room at my desk, the slice of brain on a small dish next to me. I flicked through my neuropsychology textbook, but it got me nowhere.

At that point in time, I was suffering from a bout of despair about consciousness. Psychology as a field of study was attempting to consolidate its foundations through as scientific an approach as possible. For a long time, behavioural observations were the only reliable source of psychological data; everything else was considered part of the 'black box' of the human mind. Gradually, however, thought and feelings became more of a line of enquiry. You could uncover thoughts with lists of questions (highly unreliable though they were); emotions could be measured from all kinds of bodily changes such as heart-rate and skin conductivity; and over the past twenty years the field of neuroscience had kept growing in popularity.

It was all very interesting, but I yearned for a theory about the nature of consciousness that went beyond simply pointing to brain activity. This seemed like circular reasoning to me, but you had to be careful of expressing such a desire for some kind of holistic perspective, as before you knew it you would find yourself lumped together somewhere with the New Age nut jobs and the Cartesians, or, worse still, Creationists...

Nevertheless, it became a minor obsession of mine. I devoured everything I could find on the subject of consciousness, which caused me to miss most of my regular classes. The end came when I read *The Consciousness Recording Studio*, an infamous book by American neurologist and philosopher, Antonio Corazón. According to the press, Corazón compared consciousness to a series of noise signals. This was superficially true, but in reality it was far more complex. He began with a noise-based analogy: in order to record and play back an entire orchestra, you didn't need a device which could emulate each individual instrument. Instead, using the Fourier transformation technique, an analysis of the sound spectrum could be made, and this could then be recorded as a signal onto vinyl or magnetic tape, or, these days, digitally. Then by playing this signal through a loudspeaker membrane, it was converted back into sound. So far, so clear.

What Corazón proposed was that a spectrum of brain activity at a certain point in time could be turned into a data signal using a similar process. This signal, also known as the 'consciousness signal' of the book's title, could then, as he put it, be tapped and recorded and subsequently decoded again. This essentially suggested someone's consciousness could be 'read', and that this output could, for example, be displayed in the form of a hologram.

I didn't understand a fucking word of it. Every page was packed with scientific formulae and somehow everything was explained using the Many-Worlds interpretation of quantum mechanics, and ultimately I spent more time looking for explanations of the basic terminology on Wikipedia than on reading the book itself. After two and half chapters, I gave up, temporarily cured of my consciousness obsession, but frustrated and lost, and none the wiser for it. This slice of brain brought it all back again.

*

Fina came into the bathroom while I was brushing my teeth.

'Had a good night with Brain?'

She began taking off her makeup with a wet wipe. I spat, rinsed my mouth.

'Yeah, so great, thanks for introducing us.'

'You've thrown it away though, right?'

'Can you just do that?'

'It'll stink!'

'Yes, but...'

'What?'

We had been housemates for two years and been through a lot together, but I wondered, how well did I actually know Fina? So often she would say or do something so bizarre I'd end up feeling like *I* was the one with a screw loose.

'But it's a piece of someone's brain,' I said, as if talking to a child. I could tell my tone bothered her, but it really was ridiculous to have to even explain this to her. 'It's a piece of a dead body. So, isn't it seriously illegal to just, you know, chuck it in the bin?'

'OK. How about we invite some people over, put out a nice spread, arrange some flowers, I can give a speech, you can give a speech, then we can cremate it and scatter its ashes in the canal. Will you get rid of it then?'

Also, I felt it was a shame to get rid of the brain slice so quickly. The fridge was off limits as a morgue, but it was winter, so perhaps if I wrapped it up in tin foil then it might be OK for a while; as long as I turned the heating off in my room and left the window open. If I felt cold, I could just put an extra jumper on, or make a hot water bottle. Just for one night, then I would see how things looked in the morning. In any case, was it actually legal to throw out human remains as general waste? Surely it would have to be disposed of separately. Was it organic waste — or something else entirely?

Pedro called to say goodnight. He didn't like sleeping at mine: he said that he didn't feel like 'spending the night listening to your housemate fucking' all because one time we had heard Fina with a one-night stand she had brought back. At the time, I'd suggested we drown it out with some fucking of our own. So, when we did sleep together, it was in the house his parents bought him. He often dropped heavy hints about me moving in, but I didn't see it working out as we were only six months into the relationship. Maybe I'd never come around to it.

'Did you have a good day?'

I decided to say nothing about Brain. Pedro was barely halfway through his law degree — after five years of studying — but, as soon as he disagreed about something, he would start lecturing you like a lawyer in a Hollywood film. I knew there was something wrong with what I had in my possession, and I didn't need him going off on one. I wasn't in the mood.

'What about tonight?'

'Just a bit of reading. You?'

He began a long story about an incident in the dressing room of his volleyball club. My mind began to wander immediately, which had been happening more and more. I found it extremely difficult to see the world from his perspective. There were a huge number of things I admired about him, but increasingly he felt like a stranger to me. It was not just how he approached his studies, but also his general indifference and laziness. What was going on in his mind? Did he have a good set of brains, I wondered?

Later, in bed, the childish side of my mind awakened in the darkness. What if the ghost of the person whose brain had been sliced up was angry and came looking for me in the middle of the night? How would I like it if my brain had been cut into pieces and a bit of it taken by some undergrads back to their digs?

Better not to dwell on the fact that it had belonged to a human at all. I should try not to imbue it with any personal qualities.

But it had been a human being. Perhaps a young woman, around my age, who had drowned after some heartbreak; or a senile elderly person who had died childless; a middle-aged man who had fled the Middle East, surviving the difficult journey to the Netherlands, only to succumb to an inflammation of the lungs just as he was settling into an asylum centre. Someone with a history. What was stored inside? A childhood memory carefully locked away? Images of their 'first time'? The mind's-eye video recording of a wedding maybe, or an annoying tune they had spent three agonising weeks trying to get out of their head? The brain was now out of the person's head, but was the tune really out of the brain? The matter itself was dead, but could the memories stored within it be revived or somehow retrieved? If so, who was it who would be reliving these memories, and to whom would they subsequently belong?

I was woken by several loud bangs in a row coming from outside. I shot up in a flash. Fireworks. I liked December for its cold, the holidays, the long cosy nights with warm firesides and Christmas lights, but hated the fireworks. I also felt oddly sorry for the month itself, as if there was nothing it could do about them either. I walked over to the window. There were four of them, one carrying a plastic bag and handing them out to the others. Then the flicker of a lighter: a fuse was alight. One then held onto the firework for as long as he could in a stupid act of bravado before then letting go, causing it to explode not long after leaving his hand with a bang so loud it was if it could be heard from here to Afghanistan. If only it had happened just a few seconds earlier...

Even these guys had brains. They used them to watch the world go by, practice motor skills, and laugh at one another moronically, but how often did they use them to actually think?

According to Corazón, the 'consciousness signal' was a kind of radiation, the nature of which we didn't yet understand and which we didn't yet know how to measure. We might try searching for it, but it would eventually come down to some random discovery. You couldn't control serendipity; all you could do was create the conditions in which unsought phenomena might reveal themselves.

Imagine if a device was invented ultimately which could tap into your consciousness the way Corazón proposed. What would happen if you attached it to one of those firework-worshipping halfwits?

It was 2:30 a.m. and now my heart was racing out of a combination of exasperation and agitation. I had no important commitments the next day, I could easily skip my morning lecture, but I just wanted to get some sleep. Nothing was working.

It was extremely cold. Or that's how it felt outside the warmth of my bed, by the window, slightly open for the sake of Brain. I put on two pairs of used socks, one over the other, wrapped myself in a woollen blanket and slunk off to get a drink. A tea would have been great, but the kettle always made such a racket and Fina's room was between mine and the kitchen. I didn't want to wake her. I wanted to be alone.

In the cupboard, I found the bottle of Glenfiddich I had been given for my birthday three months ago, untouched and still in its case. I didn't really drink spirits, but for now this appeared to be my only available option.

Back in my room, I decided to close the window; the slice of brain was wrapped and insulated, after all, and I settled down into the comfy, old armchair with the bottle, and a glass, next to the foil package. At first, the burn of the whisky was hard to bear. The more I drank, the smoother it slipped down.

Had there ever actually been a brain study of thoughts about thoughts? People certainly spent a lot of time on them, as well as on dredging up memories. You often heard that twenty-first century

Westerners didn't spend enough time living in the 'now', that they were too preoccupied with planning and anticipating the future and above all thinking back on bygone days, reviewing and rethinking, torturing themselves with scenarios and ideas of what might be or have been...

Perhaps the brain slice contained such thoughts; the twenty-something owner of the brain, remembering something from when she was seventeen. Maybe she had remembered that her seventeen-year-old self had also spent a lot of time thinking, and this seventeen-year-old self thought of an event that happened when she was eight. The event remembered, the memory remembered, and thus the second-order memory was etched into this slice of brain. How many of such meta-layers might a brain hold? When was the hard drive full?

And when, after much hesitation, you made a decision, what about all your alternative scenarios and doubts? Were they stowed away somewhere? Even after you burn something, you're still left with ash.

What about humour? Where would you find humour, or irony? Could you observe irony in the brain? Or was this a more serious piece of brain, the section where sadness, mourning and depression were found? I felt the same occasional panic that had gripped me since the age of eighteen or nineteen: this was it; this was all that life was. I wasn't waiting for God but rather some sort of answer. The brain slice couldn't lie, just like a new-born baby can't lie, but also neither one had any way of making itself understood. Or not yet, at least.

Even after three sizeable glasses of whisky, I couldn't get to sleep. I put on my headphones, flicked through the playlists on my phone and opted for Eels. All the bells and vibraphones, those sing-song synths reminded me of lullabies and by the third track I was out.

But not for long. This time, I was woken by a strange sound. The music had stopped and been replaced by a continuous drone — a cross between a beep and a buzz. I picked up my phone from beside the foil-wrapped slice of brain, which had been my companion for the night, but the battery was dead. The tone was coming from somewhere else. I took out my headphones: the noise stopped. I put them back in. There it was again. Maybe the headphones were faulty.

The tone grew louder and louder. It wasn't a noise in the accepted sense of the word. It was as though I could *smell* the sound; I could almost taste its colours. I felt it in all my nerve endings; like it was Braille for my fingertips and toes. These are impotent metaphors, used to describe an experience for which the right language has yet to be found. All languages that have ever tried have ever failed, mine too will fail.

I was about to remove my headphones again so I could get to sleep when I saw the door. Not the bedroom door leading to the hallway but a new door, in the wall where my desk was, and, without standing or even getting out of bed, I found myself walking towards it. It opened into darkness, but somewhere in the distance a blue light was flashing, getting closer and closer, and the siren was perhaps something I dreamt up myself. It wasn't a ghastly siren, a prophet of doom, but rather sweet, and seemed to be singing a children's song.

A man in a faded smock walked along in a pair of clogs, pushing a handcart filled with potatoes. He saw me, smiled, exposing his broken teeth and tossed me one over. Once in my hand, the potato turned into a ring, a very plain ring, not made of real gold. It glistened with a drop of moisture and I slid it onto my finger. Then my hand landed tenderly in another. An older hand, with liver spots covering its thin, wrinkled skin. I gently pinched it, but there was no response.

I sensed a long journey, at the end of which I became aware of an endless snowy landscape, so white that it hurt my eyes. A feeling of bitter cold came over my cheeks. A toddler on a sled, then a young boy on skates, followed by fresh green spring expanses, white butterflies and the summery scent of thyme fluttered through the scene, and then another long journey.

The events and images seemed to have no connection with each other, and yet I felt a coherence between all of them, and while the limitations of language now force me to list them one by one, in that moment they didn't come one after another, but all at once, and not in a confusing chaos of cacophony, but in perfect, harmonious order, like a symphony.

Many more followed. I can't remember them all now, but when someone in a white robe came to my bedside and drove the needle into my skin, I woke up feeling exhausted. I removed my headphones, pressed my phone, now working, and saw from the time that it would soon be morning. When I placed it back on the pillow, something cold rolled over onto my hand; the slice of brain, wrapped in tin foil. The idea of a dead body part, lying next to me in bed made me feel sick, and I threw it as far across the room away from me as possible.

It was light when I woke up again. It felt as though someone had put my brain through a food processor. In the back of my throat was the taste of smoked bacon. Could you actually burn your vocal cords by drinking whisky?

I sluggishly made my way to the kitchen. Fina fixed two bowls of yoghurt with granola for us. We ate side-by-side on the sofa as we watched morning TV.

I asked if she could give me any vital stats for Brain: age, gender, nationality; the fundamental facts of a human life.

'You threw it out, right?'

'Of course. Just curious.'

'Hmmm.'

She picked up the remote and turned up the volume of the TV. A chef was busy preparing a meal, a piece of meat sizzling in a frying pan. It sent a shiver through me.

'Well?'

'What?'

'Have you got anything or not?'

Fina's gaze remained fixed on the screen, her eyebrows knotted in an effort to hold her concentration.

'It's anonymous, you know that.'

'Oh come on, it must be written down somewhere, right? In a database somewhere, or on a permission form?'

'Not a clue.'

'Can't you find out?'

With an aggressive press of a button the noise of the TV suddenly stopped.

'Listen, I'm only going to tell you this once, but I can't. Even if I knew how to get hold of that information, I wouldn't do it. I'd be in serious shit.'

'But don't you have to know what kind of brain you're studying as part of your research? Young or old, male or female, sick or healthy...'

'It would go against all ethical protocol if I told you.'

'But you smuggled it out of the lab! Is *that* allowed?'

'I should never have done that. It was stupid of me. I just thought you'd find it interesting. Purely scientific.'

She got up, throwing the remote onto the sofa next to me.

'I didn't realise you'd get so fucking obsessed. You need to chill, you're giving me the creeps.'

A stamp of feet and the slam of a door. People always get angry when you point out inconsistencies in their behaviour. She was right, though. I would never know, now making that sliver of brain an orphan of sorts: no body, no identity; not even the most basic personal information.

In the shower, I recalled stories of people with old-fashioned amalgam fillings that picked up radio signals. Utter nonsense, of course, and I concluded that the previous night had been a lucid dream on which the influence of alcohol could not be underestimated.

It was a slightly underwhelming explanation, but nothing better came to mind. Anything else didn't bear thinking about. Dream or not, however, something had changed in me. History teaches us ideas can cause revolutions, so why couldn't a dream be considered a life-changing event? Whether something has really happened or is a hallucination makes little difference to the brain — the activity involved in both is the same.

The exact nature and scale of the change the dream had provoked in me was something which at that moment I couldn't fully comprehend. What I did know, however, was that I needed to remove the slice of brain from the house. I had grown superstitious because of it and didn't want to be. I pondered cremating it in the kitchen or on the balcony, but I knew that then I would never be able to go to those places again without being reminded. Imagine the smell! You couldn't just burn people, or parts of people. It had to be buried.

The heat of the air pumping out of the tram's heating system was so hot I could have fainted. Passengers fanned themselves with hastily-removed gloves to cool themselves down. The odour of thawing bodies dissipated throughout. I took off my scarf and unbuttoned my coat. In the right pocket of my jacket, I felt the tin foil.

I could have shut out the other passengers with my headphones, but I still didn't dare. This made the journey much longer and when I finally disembarked, I was hit by such contrastingly cold air that it gave me a headache.

There was still a fair old walk from the tram stop to the cemetery. The path followed the river; a biting wind brushed the surface of the water, numbed my cheeks and caused my nose to run.

I spent about an hour searching for a suitable spot. I found a nice-looking headstone with a man's name, the same birth year as me, but a date of death from a few years ago. So young... he deserved some company.

I squatted down to dig, my limbs numb. The winter earth was hard, bending the handle of the serving spoon I had brought along. Every now and again, I looked around, scared somebody might see me here rooting around in the dirt. It didn't need to be a huge grave, just a fist-sized hole would be sufficient: deep enough to conceal a piece of brain, then, when it got warmer, the soil would simply melt back into place.

When I'd hacked out a hole large enough, I removed my right glove and retrieved the brain slice from my coat pocket. I wanted to add a little ceremony to the send-off and had intended to kiss the slice, but I realised I would be kissing a poorly-wrapped and decomposing body part and so decided against it. I placed the slice of brain into the hole and, though I was not at all religious, made the sign of the cross.

I always felt the saddest part of funerals was departing, leaving the dead in the ground. Sweltering in summer, stone cold in winter, always alone.

I pushed the hacked-up earth back into the hole and stood, bowed and turned around and headed for home. Limbs stiff, a little mournful, but happy — as one should be after a funeral.

THE TOURIST BUTCHER

The man from the reception desk shuffled along in the direction of the lift, dragging my suitcase behind him. His skin was so thin and grey, like a sheet of newspaper, that he looked almost dead, with cold reptilian eyes and dark purple lips. When I shook his hand, his body had no noticeable warmth to it, just a cold clamminess.

The journey to the fifth floor lasted only seconds but what tough seconds they were. His breath smelled earthy, his gaze was fixed on the lift buttons. I didn't dare look at Xaillong, for fear that we would burst out laughing from nerves.

The room had a run-down but pleasant look. You could hear the sound of the nightlife on the street outside, but muffled enough for us to be able to sleep, and afforded a view of the church, a canal, a couple of charming little bars.

Anything else we needed?

Not right now.

The receptionist mumbled his name, followed by something else that I also missed. He said we could always call him by pressing nine on the room phone. Then a wrinkled smile as he shuffled out of the room, closing the door with a bang. Xaillong and I collapsed onto the bed with a loud, exhausted groan. Finally alone, after twenty-four hours of taxi drivers, airport staff and fellow travellers.

'I can hardly believe we're here,' he said.

It had been one of those days: bad turbulence during the long flight, problems with our luggage at the airport, and, as soon as we got through customs, we were accosted by a swindler who offered us a ride before we had even left the terminal building. He walked us round the official taxi rank in a huge circle, explaining his car was in the car park. No polite offer to take my suitcase for me, either.

He eventually led us to an unmarked car, and we took the motorway to the city, racing along at 150km per hour, an Arabic Beyoncé crying on the radio, before pulling up in front of the hotel with an abrupt screech of brakes. The damage was €78.90. The guidebook said it should have only cost €50 max. We were too tired to argue.

Xaillong gave him €80, as we had no change. The remaining €1.10 was too small a tip and the chauffeur spat on the ground right next to Xaillong, grinned, and then, through broken teeth, bade us farewell and told us, 'Better watch out for The Tourist Butcher.'

As the taxi sped off, Xaillong and I looked at each other.

'I heard it too...'

*

The travel forums had been full of it. The explosive rise in the number of visitors to the city had caused increasing concern among local residents and it was rumoured one of them had cracked. The most common version of the story was that he would kidnap and murder tourists, then dine on a portion of their flesh and sell the rest as 'beef' to restaurants which got a lot of visitors from overseas.

But the Internet was teeming with stories of murderous divers in the canals (a hoax apparently taken from a film), cocaine dealers selling deadly white heroine (a couple of deaths, no further developments), and a psychopath who tried to poison the drinking water.

'That taxi driver was just messing with us,' said Xaillong. He extended the handle of his suitcase and walked to the entrance of our hotel, where we were welcomed by the cadaverous concierge.

The view from our room put everything back into perspective: the city appeared friendly and inviting, peaceful even. From the safety of our fifth-floor window, we looked out over a church, surrounded by the hustle and bustle of the city. We could easily shut it out thanks to the double-glazed windows, or immerse ourselves in it whenever we chose. I knew for certain we'd be doing the latter many times over the next two weeks. It was why we had come after all: one final chance to go wild.

The rows of darling little houses did nothing to suggest the city was anything other than safe and peaceable. We were experienced travellers. We had spent the previous two summers in the US, a proper hotbed of serial killers and well-armed psychopaths, but nothing had happened. Stay alert, make sure to not do anything too risky; very little can go wrong.

At breakfast the next day, our deathly receptionist was nowhere to be seen.

'Relaxing in a coffin somewhere after the graveyard shift, probably,' said Xaillong.

A fresh-faced young man in his early thirties had taken his place.

After breakfast, we ventured out. The street was teeming with people trudging along the pavements, cars racing past. We decided to cross the road during a gap in traffic and were overwhelmed by a squadron of cyclists and the dinging of dozens of angry bells.

'Fucking tourists.'

We retreated again to the safety of the pavement and when our legs stopped trembling spotted the zebra crossing a little further along. Then among the other tourist hordes, easily identifiable by the very same fear, eventually made it over the road.

*

Contrary to its image as a chilled-out weed smoker's paradise, the city was anything but relaxed, and certainly not welcoming. We were snubbed at bars, ignored in shops, treated like morons in museums and otherwise regarded as a pair of walking wallets. If we stood still in the street, even for a moment, we were barraged from all sides by hurried pedestrians and a constant stream of sighs and tuts, as if the city itself was permanently annoyed. We waved at a group of school children sitting on a bench along the edge of the canal as we passed them in a tour boat and all we got in reply was a bouquet of middle fingers.

Then there was the relentless humidity. Yet the city was certainly beautiful. The tourist sites were everything we had hoped for and the food — oh the food! — was to die for. You could get anything and everything. On the first afternoon, we ate the most wonderful Italian paninis, then terrific Vietnamese spring rolls from a stall near the city hall. In the evening, we ate Surinamese pancakes with chicken curry, potatoes and string beans. And so it went over the days that followed: different cuisine for every meal. Exquisite Thai curries and Indian kormas, Argentinean steaks and Chinese noodles, Indonesian *rendangs* and all you-can-eat sushi, tapas and tagine... We gorged ourselves. We couldn't get enough. And if we fancied a snack in-between meals, which we often did, we would go to a kind of fast food place where we could treat ourselves to croquettes, sausage-esque things called '*frikandel*' and all manner of deep-fried treats from a wall of warm boxes for a couple of euro a piece. A dangerous discovery for people with our physique. We went twice a day. After the holiday we would be eating less and making healthier choices, both for us and for the little one we were planning to bring into the world.

Despite two years of marriage we were still not completely in sync. Without prior discussion, we had each bought a different travel guide. Their restaurant suggestions differed wildly but agreed on one place in particular that went by the name of Heaven. Heaven was, it turned out, close to the main street and within walking distance from our hotel. Very rarely has an establishment chosen such a suitable name.

There's steak, and then there's *steak*, and at Heaven we were served the *steak of all steaks*. It was so good it made me feel sorry for vegetarians and vegans who would be missing out — unbelievers who might let heaven simply pass them by! We ate in reverent silence, one of us occasionally uttering some brief word of exaltation.

'Incredible...'

'Jesus Christ...'

'Extraordinary...'

It made us forget how we had stuffed ourselves so divinely already during the starter on a scarcely believable quantity of wonderful *fruits de mer* presented on a three-tier platter. Even on such a full stomach, we could find room for steak as incredible as this.

We wasted nothing. And still we craved more. Delightful-looking chocolate cakes headed to other tables; sorbets crying out to be sampled, and sumptuous pink mousse of which I would happily have taken a few mouthfuls. But we finally demurred and the coffee was served to us by an older gentleman with shoulder-length grey hair that at one point had likely been blonde. He placed two small, chilled glasses on the table in front of us and, with a flick of the wrist, filled them with a cherry-red liqueur. We protested, but he assured us the drinks were on the house. 'It must be off,' I mumbled to Xaillong, but I was proven wrong. It was glorious. I should have had more faith.

'I'm Peter, by the way,' he said, in English.

I shook his outstretched hand and introduced myself, Xaillong doing the same.

'Where you from?'

We told him.

'Oh, I love your country. Sorry, I mean, I've never been there. But I never had any trouble with people from there,' he said, with a thick Dutch accent. We nodded, grinning like idiots, trying to convince each other of our mutual good intentions. Peter explained he was the restaurant's owner and chef. He apologised for the inexperienced waiting staff; due to staff illness, he had had to bring in external help. We brushed off his apologies. The food had been so phenomenal we would barely have noticed if the restaurant had been on fire.

'And what plans did you have in the city?' Peter enquired.

Celebrating. Eating and drinking whatever we pleased, one last time before returning to a healthy, responsible life. We had also come for a bit of culture, of course.

Well, people who know how to appreciate good food were always welcome, Peter told us. Would we be coming back again?

We felt obliged to say yes, particularly after the free *digestifs*, though there were at least ten other restaurants in our guidebooks we also wanted to try. Peter filled our glasses again. Eventually the restaurant closed and we stumbled back to our hotel, where the pale face of The Count, as we had taken to calling him, greeted us again, this time with an expression of pure contempt.

*

It was also a city of wheels. Buses, trams and metros, souped-up scooters and revving motors. There were 'beer bikes' everywhere: bars on wheels with a whole row of pedals under the seats, popular with stag parties. Idiots on Segues, children on scooters, teenagers, and men going through a midlife crisis, on skateboards. Those who really couldn't be arsed could be driven around in a horse-and-carriage. And punctuating all this were the ubiquitous bicycles, with the occasional racing or mountain bike scattered in between.

Perhaps a bike ride would make the heat more bearable today, we considered, what with the wind in your hair and all? There was a hire place on the corner near the hotel. They made copies of our passports, we filled in forms and I realised I had mislaid my credit card. Xaillong suggested we had perhaps left it in Heaven the night before. It must have completely slipped our drink-addled minds.

We could cycle by on our way around the city? This seemed a great idea to me, not least because we might be able to enjoy a morning snack if the place was open. It was an hour since breakfast and I was already ravenous.

We used Xaillong's card to pay for the bikes and we were given a few instructions.

'First day in town?' asked the man at the hire place.

We'd been there a few days.

'Enjoying it?'

A lot. With the enthusiasm of school children giving a presentation to class, we neatly summed up the main sights we had 'done', praised the hole-in-the-wall fast food places with their croquettes and *frikandels*, and, to prove we didn't just eat things that came out of a deep-fat fryer, described our divine meal in Heaven.

'Really?'

'You bet.'

The owner of the bike hire told us he wouldn't eat in a restaurant like that.

A restaurant like that?

'Yeah, you know, one of those places in all the guidebooks. It's a tourist trap.'

But the food was incredible?

'Sure, but. Well — have you heard about The Butcher?'

He took his hand and made a cutting motion over his throat like a butcher's knife. His fingers were black with grease. He didn't want to alarm us or anything, but...

Yes, we'd heard the stories. But they were just urban legends. He wasn't so sure. In any case, he wasn't prepared to risk it. Restaurant kitchens were dark and shadowy places. Where did the meat come from? How could you be sure?

How bad was all this really? Surely we were safe on the streets at night?

'Well...' He hesitated. 'The police say there's no hard evidence. But that's the police for you, right? All part of keeping potential damage to this city's reputation to a minimum. If I were you, I'd watch out.'

It didn't take long to cycle to Heaven, but even so by the time we arrived we were sweating like pigs. It wasn't just the heat, additionally the alcohol from the night before was trying to get out of our systems and our easy-to-spot rental bikes made us even greater targets for ridicule, irritation and rage, which did little to cool us down.

We found Peter sweeping the pavement in the morning sunshine. He was wearing a polo shirt and jeans and still seemed to have plenty of energy, though it must have been a short night for him too.

'Oh, I've been expecting you', he said as soon as he spotted us. We got off the bikes and chained them up nearby.

'Take a seat. What a lovely sunny day. Coffee? I'll go grab your card, it's in the safe. You left it here...'

We had actually been planning on visiting the natural history museum, but it could wait — natural history wasn't going anywhere. The thought of a cup of coffee and a glass of water was just too hard to resist.

We took a seat on the terrace, thumbed through our guidebooks a little until Peter returned carrying a tray supporting three cups of coffee, a carafe of cold water with mint and ice, glasses, a dish of bonbons and two small dishes of the pink mousse we had lusted after the night before.

'I did see the two of you eyeballing these yesterday, didn't I? But you couldn't fit it in?' he said, with a wink in his voice. 'Well, these were left over. Enjoy.'

It was raspberry mousse, so light and airy that every bite seemed to evaporate as soon as your tongue pressed against the roof of your mouth. A taste of childhood, of the sweets that you used to eat, but with a little body to it too. A dash of alcohol, perhaps.

Peter sat with us and drew out a couple of beautiful cycle routes by hand. 'A nice little place that — they do dinner, French cuisine, very well prepared, and they have a terrace on the waterfront. Then once you've finished eating, cycle back to the centre, along the river. That'll both perk you right up and wear you out at the same time. You'll sleep like a baby once you get back to your hotel, believe me.'

'We'll just have to hope not to bump into The Tourist Butcher when it gets dark...' I joked.

The smile dropped from Peter's face.

'Sorry,' I said. 'Was that inappropriate?'

'No, but it's not so funny. In the last few months turnover has dropped at least a third.'

'That much?'

He nodded.

'Why? Do people think it's you?'

He burst out laughing, a slight bitterness in his voice. 'If only — then at least I'd have got *something* out of it! No, they just think my meat comes from that maniac. People find that worse. They never really fear or foresee they might die themselves, they can't imagine it. But eating another human being's flesh? The idea alone is enough for them to avoid my restaurant all together. Some rival spreading rumours, no doubt.'

He jumped up.

'Come, I'll show you how it works here — how we run the place so well.'

We said there was no need, we had complete faith in him, but he insisted. His professional pride was at stake.

We followed him into the restaurant. Inside was dimly lit. The uncovered tables and lack of any candlelight or guests looked unwelcoming, so different from the night before. Peter went ahead of us into the open kitchen.

'As you can see, this is my spot, but, truth be told, it's a little for show. The real work goes on down here. Follow me.'

We followed him down the stairs and a vague intuition whispered that we were perhaps doing something very unwise.

But I dismissed it as ungenerous and in any case there were two of us and only one of him. We both had a hefty build, while he was built like a stick insect. He looked completely harmless and seemed utterly charming.

Downstairs Peter switched on the fluorescent lights, revealing a vast kitchen space, dazzling clean as far as I could see, with tiled walls, along which stood steel-finished counters, and a huge island in the middle.

'I trained all the guys who work the night shift here myself. Every evening I'm constantly going up and down, just to keep an eye on what's happening down here. Here we have the dumbwaiters, which carry finished dishes upstairs. Then over here, we have Aladdin's cave.'

He pulled open a heavy door leading into a cold store. On the shelves were crates filled with fruit and vegetables and all sorts of different ingredients but the most striking thing was the sides of meat, hanging on hooks from a rail at the back of the room, like anatomical specimens on a coat rack. It made it easy to move meat out of the cold store. Peter gave us a demonstration.

'This is where your steaks came from. A wonderful piece of beef, isn't it? And over here this is lamb, you see?'

I shook my head and dared not look. I loved meat, but just as you don't want to contemplate that your expensive dress was stitched by a child in Cambodia under appalling conditions, you don't want to contemplate those cuts of lamb you're eating were once bounding happily through the fields on four legs.

'So,' said Peter. 'Now the time has come to kill you.'

There was an awkward silence.

Then his eyes twinkled.

'I'm kidding, guys. We have to laugh about these things, right? Come on, let's go back upstairs, I'm holding you up.'

We laughed, partly out of relief, I noticed. The uneasy feeling hadn't disappeared completely, at least not for me, and it was a weird joke to make. At the same time, I felt ashamed about my suspicions: it seemed I too was caught up in hysterical newspaper headlines and ridiculous internet horror. Apparently I could no longer trust a kind and friendly fellow human, even if he was a little odd.

Perhaps in an effort to make up for my feelings of suspicion, I said, 'You know, if I were to pick anyone as The Butcher, it'd be that weird receptionist at our hotel. Xaillong and I call him The Count.'

Back outside, the sun was still shining so mercilessly it made me long to be back in the freezer.

'Well,' said Peter, 'joking aside, I think it probably is someone in the hotel business. Think about it: Someone like that knows exactly when the guests are out, so they can go into the rooms and rummage around to find out where they've been going. He can give them tips, so he knows exactly where they'll be, and haven't you noticed the victims always seem to disappear on the last days of their trip?'

'Why would that be?' asked Xaillong as he unlocked his bike.

'Well, there are plenty of theories. Nobody knows for sure. I'd keep an eye on that Count of yours, I'd say. You never know.'

We had taken our bikes out of the rack and were ready to head off again.

'Right,' said Peter, 'I'll let you go. I insist you come back at least one more time?'

'Oh you can be sure of that,' said Xaillong. 'Actually Friday is our last day. Can we book a table now?'

'Certainly. I'll save you the very best table!'

Returning to the hotel that evening after a long day out, we were more nervous of seeing The Count than before. Thankfully, he wasn't at the desk and, feeling relieved, we headed straight for bed.

Once a holiday becomes a bit of a chore, you know it's time to leave. You get a little tired having to find new places to eat every lunch and dinner, fed up of forcing yourself to be cultured all the time, less keen on experiencing new things. You need space and time, familiar surroundings, to let these new experiences sink in.

The crowds of people every day, our fellow tourists, fighting our way through swathes of selfie sticks held as menacingly as rifles. We saw the contempt in the eyes of the city's residents. We had almost come to welcome shouts of 'Fucking tourists!' as if they were a friendly greeting. Our senses were completely overwhelmed. We longed for the new life awaiting us back home. A healthy, responsible life, for what would be all three of us.

The day before we were scheduled to leave, we decided not to bother with museums and other sights but simply to go for a relaxed farewell stroll through the city. One last snack from the wall, one last spring roll from the stand, and one last, refreshing beer at our favourite canal-side bar.

At the end of the afternoon, we took a nap and packed our bags, everything but some clean clothes and toiletries. We checked in online and put on our best clothes for our final dinner in Heaven.

As we exited the lift, The Count approached us.

'Leaving tomorrow?' he said, in a gurgling whisper from deep in his throat.

Xaillong spoke for both of us.

'We are.'

'Check out is 11 a.m., don't forget.'

'We won't.'

'Please do not forget. Otherwise you will be charged an extra night.'

'Our flight is at 12:30. We'll be long gone.'

I squeezed his wrist, but Xaillong gave me two reassuring pats on the shoulder to show he had everything under control.

'You could check out now, if you want,' The Count persisted.

'No, really, tomorrow is fine. We have to go now, we have a dinner reservation.'

He pulled me outside, The Count nodding thoughtfully behind us. How long would he wait before he entered our room to rummage around in our things? Best not to think about it too long.

*

Our biggest worry about revisiting Heaven was that we might be disappointed. The food that first night had been so delightful that perhaps even Heaven itself couldn't match it.

How wrong we were.

We took it a little easier with the starter this time, so we'd have room for some more of the pink mousse. For the main course, Xaillong went for the tried and tested steak, while I went for the veal tongue in Madeira sauce. A little adventurous, but it left me just as satisfied as the steak had the first time round. Peter again served us liqueur with the coffees. Then came another round of coffees, followed by another round of liqueur, and by the time closing time came around, Peter insisted we stay on for an extra *digestif*. He had a nice selection of whisky, were we interested? Of course we were.

After the last customers had finally gone home, he came to sit with us with a bottle of single malt and three glasses.

We talked about our holiday. He wanted to know everything, what we had liked about the city, what we had disliked and we told him every detail. He nodded along in understanding, familiar with both the problems and the pleasures.

'The city sets no limits,' he said. 'With this place... all I wanted to do was open an ordinary neighbourhood restaurant. Plain and simple, but offering perfectly cooked steaks for the hard-working people, you know? Ordinary people who want to eat out every once in a while. Good food at affordable prices. Then you get included in a guidebook, then another and then another, and, before you know it, none of your customers speak your language. It's... well, don't get me wrong, customers are customers, it's no problem for me, but it's strange, you know? And no one is trying to restore the balance. The city council only listens to entrepreneurs, and entrepreneurs will keep chasing money until this city becomes one giant amusement park, where nobody actually lives and where everyone works for or exploits the tourist machine.'

He filled our glasses, trying to put us back at ease.

'It's the same in every major city, of course... at the end of the day, I'm just very happy that all these people come from all over the world to eat my food.'

We drank. Xaillong told him about our hometown, and how things were a bit crazy there too at times. For most of the year it was fine, but the good ski slopes meant it was really busy in winter. At those times we felt the same as he did, as if the city was no longer our own. He talked more and more, but I kept missing parts of it as my head sank into my arms and my eyes began to close.

The last thing I heard was Peter asking, 'Ah, you're quite drunk. How will we get you home... ?'

Everything is black. Then there's a deep, dark red. It gets lighter, the red starts to glow... all I need to do is open my eyes and look; it's as simple as that. Here we go.

Mist. Everything is hazy, Vaseline on the lenses. Yet I can hear. A dragging sound, sweeping, like the rhythmic brushing of a broom, except sharper. I won't drink that much ever again, I swear to God. How did we get back to the hotel? Did we walk? Taxi? My mind is one giant blank.

My hands? They're still asleep. I can't even rub my eyes, I have to blink away the milky haze.

'Ah, nice of you to rejoin us.'

A familiar voice. I feel I am safe.

My vision sharpens a little. A dark figure looms against a light background. It smells like a hospital. Is that where we are? Did we get so drunk we ended up in A&E? Am I really waking up in a hospital bed after a night of heavy drinking?

The scraping sound comes to a halt. The shadow bends down towards me. The heavy sound of human breathing. Without warning my face is splashed with cold water. I gasp for breath, blinking, and now all is clear.

Not the face I was expecting.

'Hi there,' the face says mockingly. 'Remember me?'

I want to shake my head, but I don't have the strength. In any case, it appears to be stuck, clamped in place, but I can't see how.

'Oh, I'm sorry. Maybe you don't recognize me without the wig.'

Out of my line of sight, he pulls something out, a bunch of shoulder-length grey hair. He waves it at me.

'I have a large collection of them now. All handmade. I learned how in a monastery. Where I learned to butcher.' He seems to take pleasure in watching my reaction to his revelations.

Only now do I notice where I am. A large tiled space, with an open stainless-steel kitchen island in the middle.

He throws the wig into a corner and returns to the worktop. He takes a large knife in one hand, a butcher's rod in the other, and gets back to sharpening, humming a tune that sounds familiar to me, a summer hit we'd been hearing all over the city

'You look a little worried. I get it. It's a strange sensation, isn't it? Don't worry though; a little paralysis. Local anaesthesia. Nothing too harmful, have no fear.'

He opens the door to the cold store. Using the rail, he pulls out a carcass hanging from one of the meat hooks.

Is it something about the limbs? The torso? Difficult to say, but somehow I know for certain it isn't a cow or pig.

'Ah. You've already guessed, haven't you?'

Xaillong is nowhere to be seen.

With skilful movements he cuts off a hunk of meat from the hip. On the steel kitchen top he trims the cut — 'We wouldn't want any gristle now, would we?' — and then walks over to me, the slice of meat on display in his open palm.

I want to throw up, but my stomach gives no response, as if I can only think the nausea and not feel it.

'Take a look at this... you can work wonders with this, you know.'

He walks back to the island and lights one of the gas rings on which he places a small frying pan, followed by a generous knob of butter. 'My god look at it go!' he shouts, clearly enjoying his work. He makes mesmerising movements, like a magician performing a trick. In goes the steak, sizzling and spattering. The smell is alarmingly familiar — like a steak cooked in butter, and yet different somehow. Unmistakably different.

'Just sear it. Add a little salt and pepper, it doesn't need anything else.'

With a meat fork he carries the steak from the pan over to a large white plate. He turns off the gas and bends down to fetch a bottle of red wine and a corkscrew. He uncorks the bottle with finesse and pours himself a glass. He comes and sits down next to me with his wine and steak, the plate in his lap. 'Cut with the grain of the meat, not against it,' he says. The first bite disappears into his mouth.

He closes his eyes and chews slowly.

I want to turn my head, but I cannot move; I want to make a run for it, but I cannot feel my arms or legs.

'Delicious. You want a piece?'

He lifts a piece to my mouth with his fork. I can clench my jaw, but I can't stop the salty-sweet aroma of butter and warm steak entering my nostrils.

'No? But just last night you were saying how exquisite you found everything.'

He shrugged his shoulders and shoved the fork into his own mouth. I cannot bring myself to imagine this piece of cooked meat and Xaillong being one and the same. I can't do it, won't do it.

'I once took a trip around Vanuatu... a group of islands in the South Pacific. Up until quite recently, they still practiced cannibalism... though, if you ask me, they probably still do to this day, but more in secret. I spoke to one of the Big Nambas... a fellow who still harboured fond memories of a cannibalistic past. He told me they ate human flesh not so much because they liked it — on the contrary, they found the taste repulsive — but rather out of anger. After killing an enemy, you ate his flesh to quell your rage. Meat marinated in anger... beautiful, isn't it?'

He sniggers and stares into the distance, as if the memory of the chief is playing on a big screen in his mind.

'I also eat out of anger. But I find I enjoy the taste. For example, just now, no frills, it tastes delightful. Add some crisp fries, or a béarnaise sauce, and now we're talking...'

A sip of wine, and he stares off into space again, as if visualising the meals, trying to evoke or recall their taste in his imagination.

'You can do so much more with human flesh. I feel I have a duty to waste as little as possible. Everything can be used, that's my motto. The hair can be made into wigs. The skin and bones make the most incredible gelatine, for raspberry pudding, for example. If you have enough genitals, you can even emulate a passable portion of *fruits de mer*. Barely distinguishable from the real thing in fact and far less chance of a bad mussel! And the wonderful things you can make with the bowels — sausages or a creamy pâté as good as any pork or goose. Oh, and the tongue I recommended you... it belonged to a fat American who talked a lot of crap about some luxury apartment she wanted to buy in the city. Adds something to the flavour, doesn't it? To know that?'

He wipes his mouth with a napkin, and with his fist to his mouth holds in a burp.

'The further it's travelled the better the taste, that's generally the way it goes for some reason. This young man, for example, came all the way from South Africa. Nice boy, beautiful body. He would have flown home last week.'

He laughs as he stands up and takes the plate over to a sink on the far side of the room.

'Anyway, to business... shall we bring him in? Now my belly is full, I can get back to work.'

The only place I've seen that kind of metal tray before was on crime shows. They use it in mortuaries. Xaillong's body is not covered with a sheet however, although he is dead, or possibly sleeping. He is being given something via a half-empty infusion bag. The wheels squeak over the sticky linoleum.

He positions Xaillong right in my field of vision, so I get a good look, and so he can study my own response.

'Do you want to say your goodbyes? A hug and a kiss might be a little tricky in this situation, but I'd take a good long look at him, if I were you. Either way, it's important you pay close attention. You will have an important job to do.'

He disappears out of sight and returns with a shiny khaki-coloured apron, made of the same material used for oilskins, material that can withstand vast quantities of fluid.

'Now, we're just going to replace this drip for you… time to gently bring you back into the realm of consciousness, my friend…'

He hooks up a new infusion bag to Xaillong's arm and sits down next to the 'bed', on the same rolling stool where he ate the steak. He then begins to stroke the naked body, his head, his shoulders, his arms…

'It's important he's calm when he wakes up, and that he feels safe. No fear at all. I sprayed myself with some of your perfume; I found it in your bag. This will subconsciously give him a feeling of trust before he opens his eyes again, and once he does open them, I have to sedate him again. Not with chemicals this time though. That would spoil the meat. No, I'll use the kind of bolt they use to stun cows before they're slaughtered, except a bit smaller. I got it online. Half-price, actually.'

I want to get out of this head, get out of it right now, or slam shut all the possible channels through which information enters.

Turn off the sound.

Disconnect my eyes.

But I have to look, I can't help it. It is as if my eyes keeping flying open of their own accord.

'Then it's simply a matter of cutting the throat and hanging him upside down until the blood has all drained out. That's when we can get stuck in with gutting him and get at that lovely set of intestines…'

He pats Xaillong's waist, on the love handles I've grabbed so many times. 'Get away from him. Get away, you filthy swine. He's my man. Get away from him.' I want to scream, but I cannot.

He composes himself, then continues. 'It's better to leave the meat to hang for a while, to mature. That makes it much more tender. For Xaillong… that was his name, right? Yes, Xaillong will need a good five days to develop some good flavour.'

He shoves his forefinger and thumb into his mouth and picks something from between his teeth. He looks at his find, a shiny brown strand of something on his glistening wet finger. He puts it back in his mouth and swallows.

'Well, now it's time for your instructions. You see, I want people to know there really is a Tourist Butcher. Not just rumours I started. It took off much faster than I thought it would at first, but soon people began to shrug it off, especially when the police started dismissing it. The number of visitors went right back up again. But that won't last for long... I'm going to cleanse this city of tourists. I want people to cancel in droves; I want everyone in the city gone. Plane, train, even bike for all I care. I want them gone. All of them.'

He resumes stroking Xaillong's hair, almost tenderly. He tilts his head and smiles.

'That's where you come in. You'll make this happen, you and your husband together. You'll sit and watch me. Then tomorrow I'll take you to the station in a wheelchair, they'll think you're a paraplegic or something. We'll take the train together, and just before we get to the border I'll leave you. By the time the anaesthesia wears off, I'll be long gone.'

Grinning slightly, he shakes his head.

'After this, I'll find a way into another restaurant. In the meantime, you'll take care of the anti-promotion of the city. Telling everyone what horrors take place here, spreading the word, like my own little evangelist.'

He falls silent, that faraway look returning. Then he seems to remember something. Looking down at his watch, his expression suddenly turns to one of irritation.

'He's taking his time, isn't he? Is he usually such a sleepyhead?'

He's looking over at me and doesn't see what I can: Xaillong's eyelids moving, fluttering cautiously.

'At least you'll survive. That's more than can be said for this little teddy bear of yours. Oh, look, here he is.'

Xaillong stretches his leg, then rolls onto his side, his back to me. I want to warn him, to scream, but no sound comes from my numbed throat, only a very soft, high-pitched tone that I don't recognise. And my eyes widen. Is this really me?

He brings a device over to the back of Xaillong's head. Then a loud metallic thud. The sound echoes through the kitchen, bouncing off the tiled walls. Xaillong's body convulses, over and over again. Then it stops.

Peter, whatever his name is, is now standing, and Xaillong's feet have been bound and roped to a steel chain. When did he manage that? Did I miss something? Was I unconscious again?

At the press of a button the chain lifts Xaillong's legs until his body is hanging upside down. The bed gets pushed out the way.

'He's still alive, you know. He's only stunned.'

Peter drags out a large, square metal trough and placed it under Xaillong's head.

Where it came from all of a sudden I do not know, but he now has a knife in his hand. It first plunges into the skin of Xaillong's throat, just below the Adam's apple. The skin dents, stretches, then bursts open under the pressure of the knife. Dark blood wells up from the cut. Peter pulls the knife towards him in one clean stroke. He hardly seems to need to use much force, the blade gliding through the pale skin and flesh as easily as if cutting through soft cheese. Then a loud hiss. The blood rushes out with all the power of a stream of urine. Xaillong almost seems to come back to life, producing a deep rumbling sound, as if letting loose a large, wet belch. Then it is over. Silence.

The blood no longer sprays, instead now splashing into the trough in gentle waves, close to where I am sitting. Perhaps it's my imagination, but I feel like I can smell it; the heavy, metallic stench. I think I can almost taste it. Or perhaps it's because I've bitten through my tongue. I feel nothing, my vision is getting hazy. In the distance, in the darkness, all I hear is his voice.

'Consider it a sacrifice... for a good cause.'

nieuw new
dutch **nederlands**
stemmen voices

VERZET is a series of chapbooks showcasing the work of some of the most exciting writers working in Dutch today, published by Strangers Press, part of the UEA Publishing Project.

Each story is beautifully translated and presented as an individual chapbook, with a design inspired by the text in collaboration with The Dutch Foundation for Literature and National Centre for Writing.

1 **RECONSTRUCTION**
   by Karin Amatmoekrim trans. by Sarah Timmer Harvey

2 **THANK YOU FOR BEING WITH US**
   by Thomas Heerma van Voss, trans. by Moshe Gilula

3 **BERGJE**
   by Bregje Hofstede trans. by Alice Tetley-Paul

4 **THE TOURIST BUTCHER**
   by Jamal Ouariachi trans. by Scott Emblen-Jarrett

5 **RESIST! IN DEFENCE OF COMMUNISM**
   by Gustaaf Peek trans. by Brendan Monaghan

6 **THE DANDY**
   by Nina Polak trans. by Emma Rault

7 **SHELTER**
   by Sanneke van Hassel trans. by Danny Guinan

8 **SOMETHING HAS TO HAPPEN**
   by Maartje Wortle trans. by Jozef van der Voort

Supported by
N National Centre for Writing
N ederlands letterenfonds
dutch foundation for literature

This series was made possible by generous funding from The Dutch Foundation for Literature